This Walker book belongs to:

Erin
_____

_____

_____

To my sister, Catherine

First published 2003 by Walker Books Ltd
87 Vauxhall Walk, London SE11 5HJ

This edition published 2011

10 9 8 7 6 5 4 3 2 1

Printed in China

British Library Cataloguing in Publication Data: a catalogue record
for this book is available from the British Library

ISBN 978-1-4063-2996-4

Mary Murphy

I Kissed the Baby!

WALKER BOOKS
AND SUBSIDIARIES
LONDON • BOSTON • SYDNEY

"I saw the baby!
Did you see
the baby?"

"Yes!

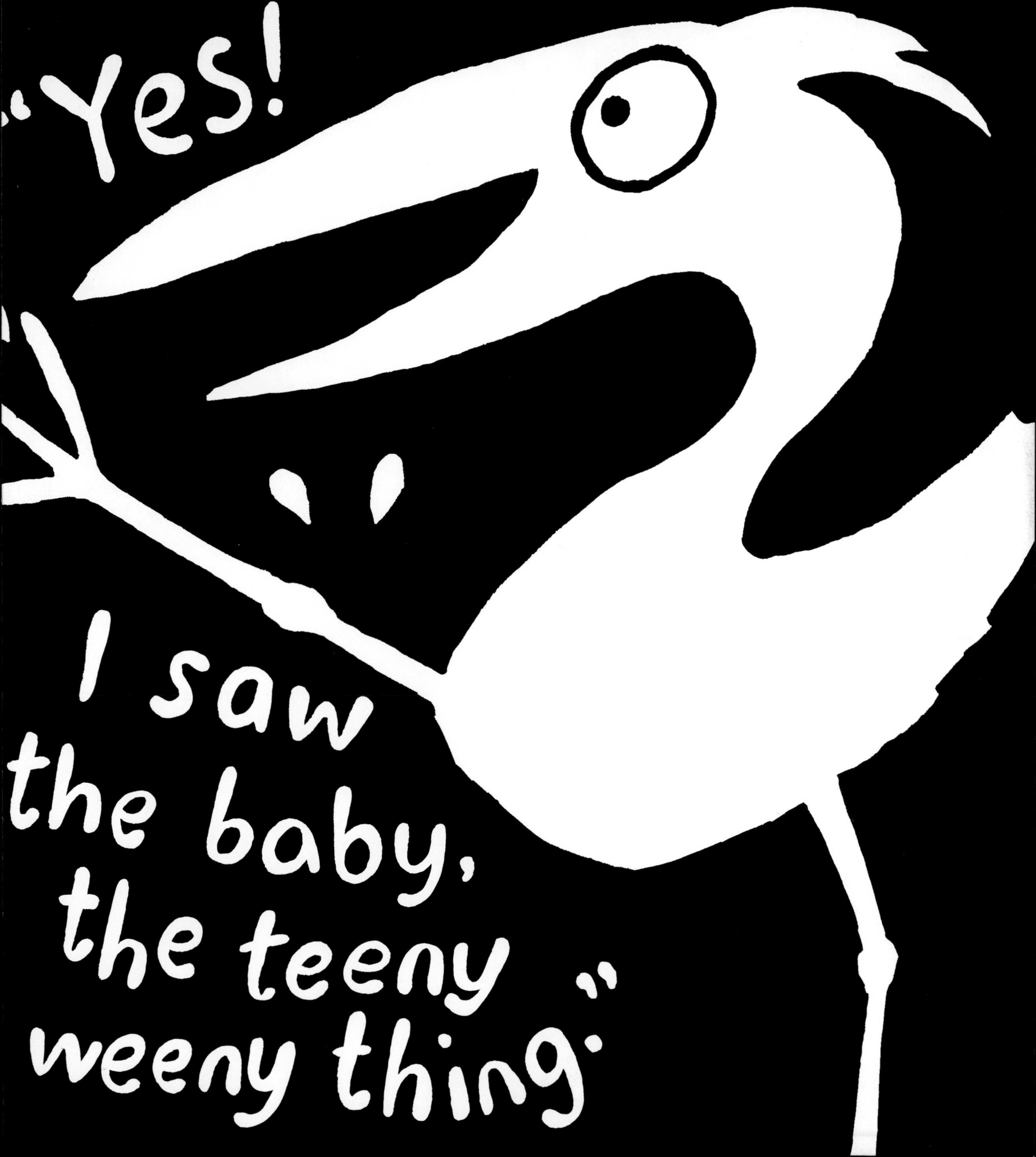

I saw
the baby,
the teeny
weeny thing."

"Yes!
I sang to
the baby, and the
baby sang to me."

"I tickled the baby!
Did you tickle
the baby?"

"Of course
I kissed
the baby!
I kissed my own
amazing baby ...

"... and I'm going to do it again!"

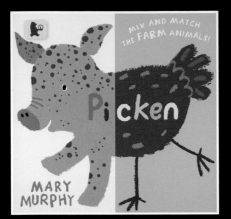
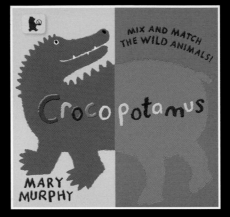

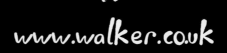